DON'T TOUCH THAT FLOWER!

For Jose, Issa, and Max. —AH

For Evie, Thomas, and Amelia. —NS

Originally published in 2023 in the UK by Scholastic Children's Books, a division of Scholastic Ltd.

ISBN 978-1-5461-2734-5

12 11 10 9 8 7 6 5 4 3 2 1

24 25 26 27 28 29

Printed in the U.S.A.   40

This edition first printing, January 2024

The sketches and full color art were created in Photoshop, with the occasional scanned paint or graphite texture added here and there.

DON'T TOUCH THAT FLOWER!

Alice Hemming   Nicola Slater

SCHOLASTIC INC.

"Hello brand new day.
Hello sunshine.
Hello lovely leaves!
Nice to see you back."

"Bird!"

Yes, Squirrel? What is it?

"It's getting very BUSY, Bird. There was a sound like CUCKOO and one like BUZZZ and a bird with a strange tail nearly flapped into my eye!"

"Well, *it* sounds like you heard a cuckoo call and a bumblebee buzz and saw a swallow. Those are all signs that spring has arrived."

"Spring...
Do we *like* spring?"

"Yes, of course."

"Then you're right, I do like spring! And, Bird, the flower is growing in between your tree and my tree...but it's a bit closer to my tree, so it's MY flower, isn't it?"

...I suppose it is, Squirrel.

"What are you doing *this time?*"

"I don't want my flower to get wet."

"But it needs water to grow. Your flower needs a shower!"

"Of course it does! Silly me!"

The morning after that...

"GO AWAY! Shoo!"

"What are you doing now?"

"That bee over there was EATING my flower! Can you BELIEVE IT?"

"No, Squirrel, the bee was collecting nectar. It's good for the flower and the bee."

"Squirrel, **I** know you love this flower, but it doesn't **really** belong to you."

WHAT? Then **whose** flower is it?

"Your flower is
a wildflower...

It's there for
everyone to enjoy."

"Still, I'm not taking any chances.

In fact, I'll keep my flower safe under here."

"Oh dear, Squirrel."

"Will it survive?"

"I hope so, but you need to give it some air and light and space."

That night...

"What have I done?
I hope my flower is all right.
I'm not going to sleep a wink."

But instantly...

ZZZZZZZZZZZZZZZZZ.

The next morning...

"WOW, Bird!

WOW!

Where did they all come from?"

Our Flowers

"Flowers don't really belong to us."

As Squirrel found out, wildflowers belong to us all. It can be fun to look
for flowers growing outside in the wild. You can enjoy them,
take photos, and draw them. When you start looking, you will find
flowers growing in all sorts of places.

Flowers are living things
"Your flower needs a shower!"

A flower is part of a plant and plants need the same sorts of things as
people do to live and grow. They need light, water, air, and food. They don't
eat like we do, though. They make their food using energy from the sun.

Flowers attract pollinators
"That bee over there was EATING my flower."

In the story, the bee was collecting nectar to make into honey.
Bees also gather pollen, which they spread to other plants as they travel
from flower to flower. This helps the plants grow. Bees are *pollinators*.
Butterflies, other insects, some birds, and some bats can also be pollinators,
and flowers look and smell beautiful to attract them.

Flowers are good for us

As well as helping plants to grow, flowers are good for us in other ways. Many insects like to feed on flowers. So do birds, animals, and even humans. Flowers can provide medicines, and they make us feel relaxed and happy when we look at them.

Be a friend to flowers

🌸 Learn about flowers. Find out their names and where they like to grow.

🌸 If you have a garden, a balcony, or windowsill, you could grow your own flowers.

🌸 Encourage people at home or school to leave part of the yard unmown so wildflowers can grow.

🌸 Make your own insect hotel.

Flowers are not the only sign of spring

Squirrel spotted a cuckoo, a bumblebee, and a swallow, which are all signs of spring.
Can you think of any more?

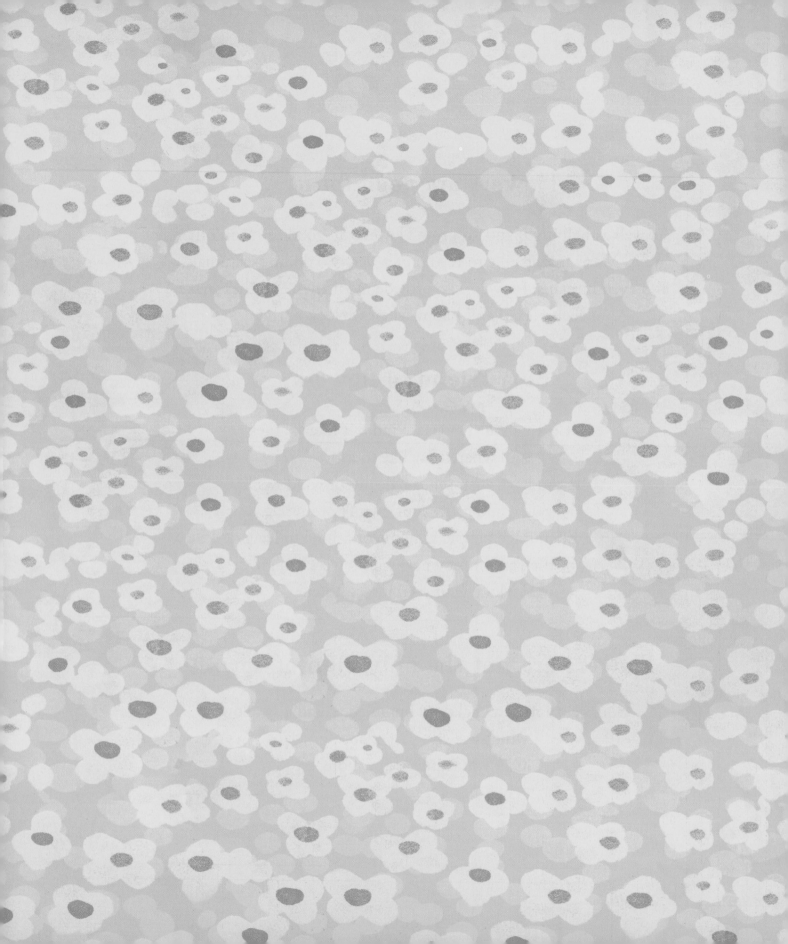